Alice Goes North

Written by **Karen Wallace**
Illustrated by Bob Dewar

A & C Black • London

To Cougar,
who might be an anteater one day

First published 2006 by
A & C Black Publishers Ltd
38 Soho Square, London, W1D 3HB

www.acblack.com

Text copyright © 2006 Karen Wallace
Illustrations copyright © 2006 Bob Dewar

The rights of Karen Wallace and Bob Dewar to be identified as the
author and illustrator of this work respectively has been asserted by them
in accordance with the Copyrights, Designs and Patents Act 1988.

ISBN 0-7136-7622-1
ISBN 978-0-7136-7622-8

A CIP catalogue for this book is available from the British Library.

This book is produced using paper that is made from wood grown in
managed, sustainable forests. It is natural, renewable and recyclable.
The logging and manufacturing processes conform to the
environmental regulations of the country of origin.

Printed and bound in Singapore by Tien Wah Press (Pte) Ltd

Chapter One

Alice was an anteater who lived in the jungle. Every day she dug for ants with her sharp, curved claws.

And every day, while the other anteaters snoozed in the sunshine, Alice read books.

One day, Alice was walking by the
riverbank, thinking great thoughts
about walking on the moon and
learning to fly.

She didn't notice Cornelius the crocodile
appear in the water.

"Hello, *Alith*," said Cornelius. He was carrying something in his mouth, so he sounded a bit odd.

"Hello, Cornelius," replied Alice, climbing quickly onto a high stone. She liked Cornelius but sometimes he forgot his manners and gobbled up his visitors.

"I found *thith* in the *reedth*," said
Cornelius. He dropped a magazine
wrapped in red plastic on the bank.
"I thought you might like to read it."

The magazine was red and green and covered in gold stars.

There was a picture of a big man with a white beard in a red hat carrying a lumpy sack over his shoulder.

Alice knew all the words except one.
"What does *Christmas* mean?" she asked.

But Cornelius had swum away.

Alice read the magazine from cover
to cover.
By the time the sun went down, Alice
knew all about Christmas.

But she had one big question…

"Why don't anteaters get Christmas presents?" Alice asked her mother at supper.

Alice's mother scratched her head.

"We'll ask the other anteaters tomorrow," she said at last.

Chapter Two

The next day, Alice's mother called
a meeting.

"Why don't anteaters get Christmas
presents?" she asked the other anteaters.

No one knew the answer.

The little anteaters hadn't even *heard* of Christmas!

"Well, if nobody knows," said Alice. "I'll go to the North Pole to ask Father Christmas himself!"

"You can't do that!" cried Alice's mother.
"It's too cold."
"It's too dark," said her aunt.
"It's too dangerous," said her
grandmother. "And it's *very* far away."

But the little anteaters kept quiet.
If Alice was brave enough to go to the
North Pole, they weren't going to stop
her. They liked the idea of Christmas
presents, too!

That night, Alice read a book about the North Pole. Her mother and her aunt and her grandmother were right! It *was* cold and dark and dangerous, and *very* far away.

It was not the kind of place for an anteater at all!

So the next day, Alice went down to the river to find Cornelius the crocodile. "May I look in your dressing-up box?" she asked. "I need clothes to go to the North Pole. All I have is my pink handbag."

Cornelius yawned and showed rows and
rows of sharp teeth.
"Help yourself," he said.

The dressing-up box was full of
wonderful things.
Alice chose a thick, woolly coat, a
turquoise jumpsuit, a green hat with
a feather and some goggles.

She was just about to shut the box when
she saw a pair of flippers. They would do
for snowshoes.

Alice put on her new clothes and stared at her reflection in the water. She looked just like a *real* explorer!

Then she made herself a raft and paddled down the river towards the North Pole.

JP/207652/

Chapter Three

It was a long way to the North Pole.
And every day it felt colder and darker
and more dangerous.

When Alice finally arrived, she was amazed – no one knew where Father Christmas lived!

"Follow the Sun," said a walrus, scratching his tail with his tusks.

"Follow the Moon," said a polar bear, chewing on a fish.

It was hopeless. There were no tracks or paths, and Alice couldn't find a bus or a sledge or a toboggan.

So Alice decided to hitchhike.
She took a compass from her pink
handbag and turned round to face
North. Then she stuck out her thumb
and waited.

Nothing happened. Nobody came by except for a white hare who asked lots of silly questions:

"Aren't you cold?"

"Why are you wearing those funny things on your feet?"
"What's an anteater doing at the North Pole?"

The hare thumped his foot and stared at Alice. "Are you stupid or something?"

"I've come to ask Father Christmas
a question," said Alice, in her most
grown-up voice.
"What question?" demanded the hare.
"Why don't anteaters get Christmas
presents?" said Alice.

The hare's pink eyes bulged and he fell about laughing.

"Father Christmas is far too busy to think about anteaters!" he squealed.

"Looking for a ride?"
A tiny man was driving a huge sledge, pulled by eight dogs and piled with parcels. He wore a furry hood and there was a big smile on his face.

"Yes, please!" shouted Alice and jumped in.

Then, before she could stop them,
tears trickled down her cheeks.
What if the hare was right? What if
Father Christmas really *was* too busy
to think about anteaters?

"Don't listen to that hare," said the tiny
man. "He's only cross because he didn't
get what he wanted last Christmas."

Alice was amazed. "How do you know that?" she asked.

The tiny man laughed. "Because he says the same thing every Christmas. Nothing is good enough for that hare!"

Alice wiped her nose on her sleeve.
"But is it true? About Father Christmas
and anteaters, I mean?"
"Ask him yourself," said the tiny man.
"We're almost there!"

Chapter Four

Alice stood in the middle of an enormous room. Hundreds of elves were wrapping thousands of presents in coloured paper. "I've come to ask Father Christmas a question," said Alice.
"Impossible," said an elf. "He's too busy right now."

Then a door painted with a red star flew open. A huge man in a baggy suit appeared. He had a long, white beard and a curly moustache and he stared straight at Alice.

"Alice the anteater!" he cried. "I've been expecting you!"

Even though his blue eyes sparkled like two sapphires, Alice wasn't fooled. This was the guy who was too busy to think about anteaters. She stood up to her full height and marched into his office.

"Welcome to the North Pole!"
Father Christmas held up two bottles.
"Red or green?"

"Red, please," said Alice firmly.
"Then I shall have green!" said Father
Christmas. He poured two glasses and sat
down. "Now … how can I help you?"

Suddenly, Alice felt nervous. She gulped at her drink. It tasted of berries and sunshine. She swallowed the whole lot and leaned forward.
"Why don't anteaters get Christmas presents?" she asked.

"Everyone else does!" she said.

"Is it true you're too busy to think about us?" she wailed.

Then she burst into tears!

"Alice," said Father Christmas gently. "If you stop talking for one minute, I'll tell you why anteaters don't get Christmas presents."
Alice looked up into Father Christmas's face. It was all blurry.
"Why?" she howled.

"Because you've never *asked*," said
Father Christmas. "That's all anyone
has to do."

Alice's mouth turned into a huge O.

"Now, jump onto one of my reindeer,"
said Father Christmas. "And you'll
be home in
the twinkling
of an eye!"

Chapter Five

Alice arrived back in the jungle on Christmas Eve. Everyone was delighted to see her. All the little anteaters asked the same question: *Why don't anteaters get Christmas presents*?

So Alice told them…

Cornelius was amazed. "Are you sure
it's as simple as that?" he demanded.
"That's what Father Christmas said,"
replied Alice. "All we have to do is ask."
"Even crocodiles?" asked Cornelius.
"Even crocodiles," said Alice.

That night, Cornelius and all the little anteaters gathered around a hollow tree trunk and pretended it was a chimney. They each wrote down the present they wanted. Then, one at a time, they pushed their piece of paper up the tree.

44

The next morning, it was Christmas.
None of the anteaters could believe their
eyes. At the foot of the hollow tree was
a huge pile of presents!

Everyone received exactly what they'd
asked for. There was even a big jar of
mustard for Cornelius!

"What did *you* get, Alice?" cried
an anteater as he wobbled past on
a brand-new bicycle.

Alice ripped open the present with her
name on it and let out a whoop of joy!
It was a box of her favourite chocolate-
covered ants. She stuffed a handful in her
mouth. They were absolutely delicious!

Then Alice had a brilliant idea. Why not send Father Christmas a present in return? But what? Alice swallowed another handful of chocolate ants and thought hard. The more she chewed, the more she thought and suddenly she had the answer…

She would send him the best thank-you
letter ever!

Dear
Father Christmas
Thank you for all
our Wonderful
Presents. Love
Alice xxx